Gulliver's Travels

Written by Andrew Matthews
Illustrated by Steve Horrocks

Collins

My name is Lemuel Gulliver. When I was a young man, I worked as a doctor in London.

But it became so difficult to find new patients that I had to go to work on a sailing ship. I left my wife and children behind in England.

One night there was a fierce and frightening storm. The ship struck a rock and began to sink.

I was terrified I'd drown, but luckily I washed up on the shore of an island.

I don't know how long I slept, but when I woke up, I found that something was terribly wrong.

3

He's moving! FIRE!

OUCH! No, it's not a dream!

I was worried that they'd seriously hurt me, so I decided to keep very still.

Maybe I can escape when it gets dark and nobody can see me.

Where am I? I'm really hungry. May I have some food?

5

But I didn't know that the juice had been mixed with something to send me to sleep. While I was sleeping, the little people loaded me on to a cart.

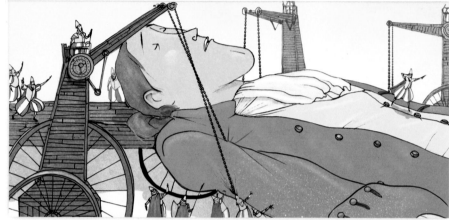

They drove me to the capital city.

When I woke up, to my horror I found I was chained up in an old building.

Then a grand-looking person arrived and I realised what was happening. They had brought me to see the Emperor of the island.

9

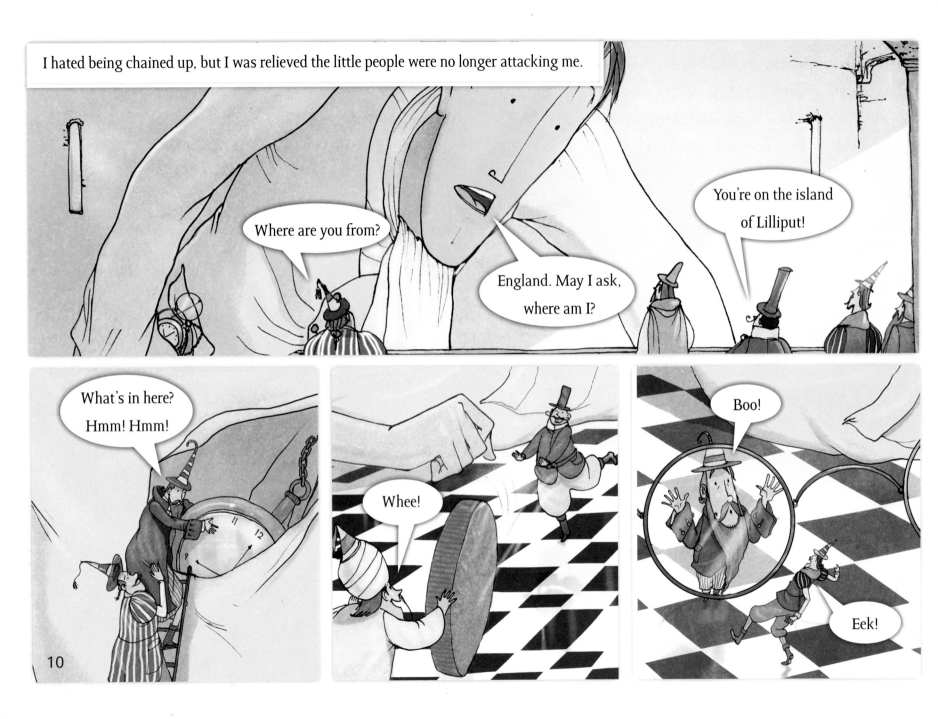

I realised that the scholars were just interested in me and the things I owned, and didn't plan to hurt me. The scholars were also very intelligent and I learnt a lot about Lilliput …

… but at night, when I was alone, I thought of my family. I was lonelier than I had ever been before.

The Emperor visited me often and told me many tales about the history of Lilliput.

We've won so many battles — isn't it wonderful?

It's strange that such tiny people can fight so many wars!

But although the people were much nicer to me now, they still kept me chained up. I knew I needed to do something to help Lilliput, in order to persuade them to release me and help me get home. One day, I got my chance …

What shall we do? A neighbouring island has declared war on Lilliput. Enemy ships are coming to invade us — and their army is much bigger than ours!

Unchain me, and I'll help you.

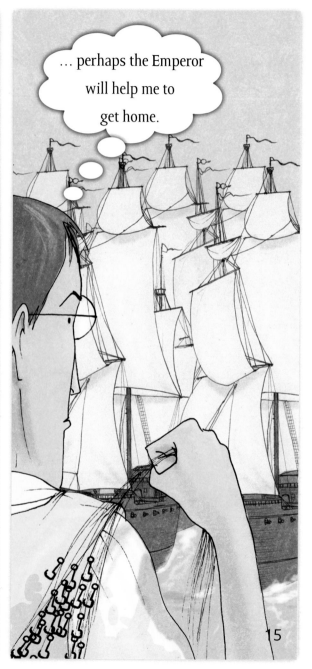

15

As I'd hoped, the soldiers and sailors on the enemy ships were terrified.

There's a giant coming this way!

How can we fight a man as huge as that?

Prepare for battle!

16

I stuck a hook into the prow of each ship …

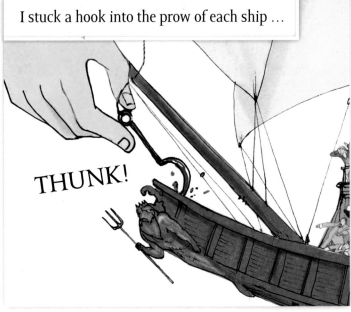

THUNK!

THUNK!

The next day, I went for a walk on my own.

I'm so lonely!

I really miss my family.

But without a ship big enough for me, I have no way of getting back to England!

19

I felt so happy at the thought of sailing home! But I needed the help of the people of Lilliput. Since I'd beaten their enemies, they agreed to do as I asked. They chopped down trees to give me the wood I needed and blacksmiths forged huge nails.

23

It was time to go. I felt a little sad to be leaving Lilliput, but I couldn't wait to get home to my family.

I was very pleased when my cattle and sheep became famous and earned me money. People came from all over the country to see them.

I just can't believe my eyes!

Aren't they sweet!

Things got even better when I sold my flock and herd to two businessmen. They paid me a lot of money!

Deal!

I'll show the cattle at country fairs, and charge a penny a peep!

My adventures in Lilliput made me a rich man and I promised my wife that I wouldn't go on any more voyages.

29

The Lond

Gulliver: shipwrecked man returns — with tiny animals!

Lemuel Gulliver had been working as a ship's doctor when the ship sank several months ago, but he returned home yesterday, alive and well. In addition to the shock of his safe return, Gulliver brought with him some very unusual animals.

The tiny cows and sheep are already the talk of the country, with people travelling far and wide to take a peek at Gulliver's miniature farm. When asked for a comment, Gulliver said, "I'm delighted to be home with my family, and to bring with me such unusual animals that have never before been seen in this country. I welcome everyone to come and visit them."

Ideas for reading

Written by Gillian Howell
Primary Literacy Consultant

Learning objectives: *(word reading objectives correspond with Lime band; all other objectives correspond with Diamond band)* continue to apply phonic knowledge and skills as the route to decode words until automatic decoding has become embedded and reading is fluent; increasing their familiarity with a wide range of books, including myths, legends and traditional stories, modern fiction, fiction from our literary heritage, and books from other cultures and traditions; checking that the book makes sense to them, discussing their understanding and exploring the meaning of words in context; drawing inferences such as inferring characters' feelings, thoughts and motives from their actions

Curriculum links: History

Interest words: patients, fierce, exhausted, juice, Emperor, scholars, persuade, neighbouring, honour

Word count: 1,230

Resources: pens, paper, art materials

Getting started

- Look at the cover and read the title. Explain that this is a retelling of a famous story written in the eighteenth century. Ask the children if they have heard of the story before and what they know of it.

- Ask them to look at the cover and speculate on what the story might be about, giving reasons for their answers.

- Ask the children to read the back cover blurb and briefly flick through the book, looking at the illustrations. Ask them how important they think the illustrations are to the story.

- Explain that this is a graphic novel. Discuss what this means, how the text is laid out and how to read this type of book with the children.

Reading and responding

- Look at pp2–3 together to ensure the children understand how to read the frames in the right sequence.

- Ask the children to read the story using a quiet voice. On p2, if the children mispronounce *patients*, ask them to reread the previous sentence and work it out from the context. Check they understand what patients are.

- On p9, if children struggle with *scholars* ask them to think of another word that begins *sch*, e.g. *school*. If they don't know what a scholar is, ask them to relate the word to *school* to work it out and discuss the link together.

- Remind the children to read the speech bubbles and use an expressive tone. Pause occasionally and ask the children what extra information about the story they learn from the speech bubbles.